Chapter One

Little Prince T Rex was busy.
He was making a big dragon's head for
Dragon Day.

His mum and dad, Queen Teena Regina and King High T the Mighty, were trying on funny dragon hats...

...and the dinosaurs were putting on funny dragon costumes.

Everyone loved Dragon Day. It gave them a chance to dress up and have fun.

'Why do we have Dragon Day, Mum?' asked Little T.

'Well,' said his mum, 'long ago a bad-tempered dragon came to the castle.

He stole your great-grandmother Princess Rexeen and wouldn't give her back.'

'What happened?' asked Little T.
'Your great-grandfather, Prince Capital T, disguised himself as a dragon and went to rescue her,' said Queen Teena.

And did he do it?

He most certainly did.

'How?' asked Little T.

He told the dragon jokes.

Jokes?

'Yes,' said his mum with a grin. 'Dragon jokes.'

Like ....
what kind of fly is too big to get through your front door?

I don't know.

A dragonfly!

Ha ha!
What did the dragon do?

'He laughed so much that the prince escaped with the princess,' said his mother.

'From that day on the dinosaurs have celebrated her escape by holding a Dragon Day. They dress up as dragons and tell each other dragon jokes.'

The costumes are meant to be funny and make the dinosaurs laugh.

Mine won't! It's going to be scary! My friends are going to help me.

Chapter Two

Little T's friends, Don, Bron, Tops and Dinah were waiting for him at the castle gates.

They had made a wonderful body for the dragon.

Little T lifted the dragon's head over
Tops, and Don, Bron and Dinah lifted
the dragon's body over themselves.

'I'll go and tell the dinosaurs there's a
real dragon coming,' said Little T.

The dinosaurs were surprised.
Little T ran towards them shouting,
'Look out! Look out!'

As the dragon charged towards them
they started to run...

...but then they stopped.
The 'real' dragon had
tripped over its tail...

...fallen in
a heap...

...and lost
its head.

'Ha ha!' laughed the dinosaurs. 'That's
the funniest 'real' dragon we've ever
seen! Well done, Little T!'

Little T glared.
It wasn't supposed
to be funny.
The dragon was
supposed to scare
the dinosaurs.

Fed up, he and his friends trudged back
to the castle.

Suddenly
Little T
noticed
something
on the
ground.

He picked it up.

'What's this?' he said.

'It looks like a little elephant's tusk,'
said Don.

'Can't be,' said Dinah. 'There are no
elephants around here.'

Perhaps it's a bit of a toy.

Little T grinned.

'Let's pretend it's a dragon's tooth!' he cried.

'We can make big dragon-shaped footprints and show them to the dinosaurs.'

They went to the edge of the forest where the ground was soft and set to work.

Using their feet they stamped out big dragon-shaped marks in the mud.

'Now for the pretend dragon's tooth,' said Little T with a grin, and dropped it beside the footprints.

Little T then rushed off to warn the dinosaurs that there was a huge dragon about.
He had the proof.

The dinosaurs didn't really believe him but they came to look anyway. They thought it might turn out to be funny again.

'There!' said Little T, pointing to the footprints and the pretend dragon's tooth.

The dinosaurs looked down...

...then they looked up into the forest.

'You're right!' they cried in panic.

There is a dragon! Run!

All the dinosaurs suddenly turned tail and ran for their lives.

Chapter Three

Little T and his friends laughed.
'We scared them after all,' chortled
Little T.

They were surprised!

But now it was their turn to be surprised.
Because just then, behind them, they
heard a loud...

WAAAAAR!

...and a dragon came out of the forest.

Everyone stood rooted to
the spot.
Little T gasped and
looked down at the
pretend dragon's tooth.
'It was real after all!' he croaked.

At that moment Little T's mum and dad came running up.

'Don't worry! I'll save you!' cried High T.

But he slipped on the muddy ground and fell.
SPLODGE... onto his face.

'WAAAAR!' cried the dragon again. His breath was like a hot wind and a little bit of smoke drifted out of his nose.

Queen Teena skidded to a halt in front
of the dragon.
'Be careful, Mum!'
cried Little T.

He might
roast you!

But Queen Teena smiled and picked up
the tooth.

'I don't think
so,' she said.
'He's the same
age as your
little sister –
just a baby!
And this is one
of his baby
teeth.'

24

My guess is that he's lost and is looking for his mother.

'WAAAAR!' wailed the baby dragon and big, warm tears dropped onto High T's head.

'Ahhhh!' sighed the king as he washed away the mud.

Just like a hot shower!

Queen Teena took the baby dragon's hand.

'Let's all go back and tell the dinosaurs,' she said.

Then we can set about finding the dragon's mum.

The dinosaurs were glad that the dragon was only a baby. But they were worried that his mum would be as bad-tempered as the dragon who stole the princess.

'But we must find her,' said Queen Teena.

A baby needs its mother.

The dinosaurs sighed and agreed.

You're right. But how can we find her?

Chapter Four

Suddenly Little T had an idea.
'Baby dragons can't fly,' he said. 'But
their mums can. So we should put
something into the sky to attract her
attention.'

In case she's flying
around nearby.

'Like what?' asked his dad.

'A dragon,' replied
Little T and pointed
to his and his friends'
dragon costume.

'How will you get that into the sky?' asked his dad.

We can't do magic and the Royal Magician is on holiday.

'We don't need magic,' said Little T.

We need hot air to make it rise like a balloon.

29

'Where on earth will we get hot air?'
asked High T but Queen Teena smiled.

'From the baby dragon, of course,' she
said.
'Isn't that right, Little T?'

That's right,
Mum.

Quickly Little T tied the head to the
body with a long piece of rope.

Then he showed the baby dragon what
he wanted him to do.

'Like this!' he said.
His friends lifted
up the costume
and Little T blew
into the head.

The baby dragon thought it was a game
and smiled.

'WAAAR!' he cried and, copying Little T,
he blew a long blast of hot air into the
head too.

Slowly the dragon costume lifted into
the sky.

But as the dragon costume bobbed high
in the air the dinosaurs began to get
worried.

But before they could do anything there
was a great rushing noise...

Chapter Five

WHOOSH!

...and out of the sky
swooped a huge dragon.

It was the baby dragon's mother.

Flames curled out of her nose and her breath was as hot as a furnace.

She looked around quickly. When she spotted the other dragon she threw out her arms.

'Babykins!' she cried.

Come to Mummy!

The baby dragon
leapt into his
mother's arms
and she gave
him a big
cuddle.

Chapter Six

The dinosaurs sighed.
'Ahhh,' they murmured.

Isn't that nice?

Then they realized they were still
wearing their silly dragon costumes.

Slowly they
began to
back away.

'Wait a moment,' said the big dragon. 'Don't go. I haven't had a chance to look at all your lovely costumes yet.'

'Of course,' replied the mother dragon.
'I love funny things.'

'Oh yes,' replied the baby dragon's mother.

'My grandfather used to tell me lots. It seems that a funny little dragon once made him laugh so much that it cured his bad temper.'

Now all dragons tell jokes!

'Well,' said Queen Teena, 'you've certainly come to the right place for jokes.'

We tell each other dragon jokes all the time on Dragon Day!

'Brilliant!' cried the big dragon. 'Let me tell you one!'

Why is a dragon like the weather in the desert?

We don't know!

'Because it's always a scorcher!' cried the
big dragon. She threw her head back
and bellowed with laughter.

'Ha ha!' she roared and flames shot out
of her nose into the sky. 'A scorcher. Get
it?'

'We do,' cried the dinosaurs, grinning.
'Now it's our turn.'

'I don't know,' said the mother dragon.

'It wanted to play squash!' said the dinosaur and once more the dragon roared with laughter.

'This is the best fun ever!' she cried. 'Babykins and I are going to come here every year!'

'Aren't we, Babykins?'

The baby dragon was playing with Little T's baby sister.

'WAAAAR!' he cried, smiling and nodding.

The dinosaurs were delighted. 'We'll have real dragons for Dragon Day!' they cried.

Thanks to you and your friends, Little T !

Little T grinned.
'It won't be scary, though, will it?' he
said.

And I liked
it when we
were being
scary.

He turned to his friends.

Perhaps next year we should look
for a monster or maybe a ghost
to invite to Dragon Day.

'Great idea!' cried his friends.
'Ha!' snorted the dinosaurs.

But Little T just smiled.
'Oh no?' he said. 'Just wait and see.'

47